STRATEGY SHOWDOWN

D1371938

Text by Thomas Kingsley Troupe
Illustrated by Fran Bueno

STONE ARCH BOOKS
a capstone imprint

Published by Stone Arch Books, an imprint of Capstone.
1710 Roe Crest Drive North Mankato, Minnesota 56003
capstonepub.com

Library of Congress Cataloging-in-Publication Data is
available on the Library of Congress website.
ISBN 9781666344721 (hardcover)
ISBN 9781666353334 (paperback)
ISBN 9781666344738 (ebook PDF)

Summary: Jae Cho doesn't have much luck at playing
games. But when she watches her brother, Dal, playing
Castle Crusaders 5, the game's various strategies
fascinate her. One day when Dal leaves the game
running on his computer, Jae can't resist playing for
herself. Before long she's hooked on the game and
secretly playing against others online whenever she
can. However, she soon accidentally enters an esports
competition in her brother's name! Will Dal be angry
that Jae has been using his computer and played
as him? Or will he help his sister dominate at the
tournament?

Editor: Aaron Sautter
Designers: Brann Garvey, Elyse White
Production Specialist: Polly Fisher

Shutterstock: Elena_Lapshina,
(pixel texture) design element

TABLE OF CONTENTS

MAIN PLAYERS

JAE CHO

DAL CHO

CHAPTER 1

NOT A GREAT GAMER

Jae Cho scanned the game board on her phone and read the letter tiles already laid out. Big words crisscrossed the board wherever she looked. Glancing down, she noted the letters she had left.

X, E, and F.

Not much to choose from, Jae thought. She glanced up from her cell phone and saw her best friend Bishara watching her while holding her own phone.

"Take your time," Bishara said, smiling. "It's not like our lunch period is over in a few minutes."

"Aaah!" Jae said, shaking her phone in frustration. "I can't take the pressure!"

Jae tapped her letter E and dragged it over each word. Even though she knew EFOREST wasn't a word, she tried it. She also tried ESPONGE, SPONGEE, and EQUAGMIRE.

None of them worked.

The letter E is supposed to be easy to use in this dumb game, Jae thought, shaking her head. She raised an eyebrow and studied the board again.

"I don't get it," Jae said.

"Do you give up?" Bishara said. "I honestly don't think you—"

"No, no," Jae said. "Give me a second. I just don't understand how you have so many points, and I barely have any!"

The score didn't lie. Jae was sitting at 46 points while Bishara was at 201.

"It's all about strategy," Bishara said. "All those bonus spaces give you more points for your high-scoring tiles. But you never do that. It's like you get so excited about a word—"

"—that I just drop it in without planning ahead," Jae said. "Ugh. You're right."

The bell rang, signaling the end of the lunch period. Students around them began picking up their trays and filed out of the lunch room.

"I guess I give up, again," Jae said. She pushed the SURRENDER button on the game app, giving her friend the victory.

"Good game," Bishara said with a smile.

"Not really," Jae said with a sigh.

"I meant for me," Bishara said, smiling.

Jae laughed. Her friend could be blunt sometimes, but Jae knew she was kidding. It was one of the things she liked about Bishara. She wasn't "fake" like so many other students in her class.

"At some point I'm going to find a game I can beat you at," Jae said. "I just have the worst luck!"

As Bishara threw her soda can in the recycling bin, Jae folded up her lunch sack and tucked it into her backpack. Then they headed down the hall to their row of lockers.

"I don't think it's bad luck," Bishara said. "I'm just really competitive. Should I let you win instead?"

Jae grabbed Bishara by the arm and tried to make the most serious face she could.

"Don't you dare," Jae said, but couldn't help smiling. "You know how much I love games. Letting me win would be like breaking some sort of gaming law. The gaming gods would NOT be happy if you did that!"

Bishara stopped at her locker and began spinning the combination dial.

"You're right," she said. "But for someone who loves games so much, you never win!"

"Ouch," Jae said, pretending to be punched in the stomach. "The truth hurts."

"Sorry," Bishara said. "But I've got to give it to you. If I lost as often as you, I wouldn't play anymore."

Jae shrugged. "Guess I just haven't found the right game yet."

Bishara fished her social studies book out of the bottom of her locker. "Have you ever actually won at anything?"

"Very funny," Jae said and then thought about it. "I think I won a game of rock-paper-scissors once."

"Oh, boy," Bishara replied. "That's kind of sad."

"Okay, quick round, right now," Jae shouted. "1, 2, 3!"

Jae chose scissors. Bishara chose rock.

"Ugh! No way!" Jae cried. "Quick, go again. Best of three!"

CHAPTER 2

KEEP IT DOWN

After school, Jae sat in her room to do her homework. She had a ritual when it came to getting her assignments done. First, she cleared away any books or papers that weren't related to what she was studying. Then, she pulled a pen, a pencil, and a worn, pink eraser from her backpack. She placed them near her left hand for easy access.

For the final touch, Jae played classical music at a low volume. Although her friends didn't like that type of music, Jae enjoyed listening to the work of geniuses as she worked to become one herself. It also helped her ignore the sounds in the rest of the house while she tried to work.

As the music started, Jae opened her school planner and pulled out her worksheets. But as soon as she began writing, she heard shouting from across the hall. It was loud enough to drown out her music. The sudden sound startled her, and she broke her pencil's lead.

Dal! Jae thought. Her older brother was, as usual, making way too much noise.

"Hey!" Jae shouted. "Keep it down in there!"

There wasn't a response. Instead, she heard what sounded like an explosion. The sound made the framed photo of her grandmother rattle on her night stand.

What is going on in there? She turned her music up a bit and clicked a new pencil lead into place. She wrote her name before Dal shouted again.

"Get outta here!" Dal shouted from his room. "You're totally using a MOD, Tim! There's no way you blasted through that!"

Jae took a deep breath to try to calm herself down.

Focus, focus, she thought.

A few seconds later, another explosion rumbled the house, loud enough for her mom to shout from downstairs.

"Dal!" Mom cried. "Turn that down! The neighbors will call the police to our house!"

Jae tossed her pencil aside and stood up. She marched to her bedroom door, threw it open, and stomped to Dal's closed bedroom door. There was a sign taped to the front. It showed two guys from the video game *SUPER FIGHTERS* who looked strong enough to snap trees with their bare hands. Beneath the characters were the words:

NO LITTLE SISTERS ALLOWED.

Whatever, Jae thought. She couldn't believe her brother was a junior in high school. He sure didn't act like it.

Jae opened Dal's door and stepped inside but was prepared to be thrown back out. Miraculously, that didn't happen.

"What is going on in here?" Jae asked.

Dal sat at his computer staring at the huge monitor he'd bought a few weeks before. He was hunched over a keyboard and mouse and leaned forward in his chair. He looked like a mad professor conducting an experiment.

Jae glanced at the screen. She saw what looked like catapults flinging rocks at castles and knights battling monsters. There was digital smoke on the screen as armies ran toward a broken and crumbling castle.

"Eat it, Tim!" Dal shouted into the microphone on his headset. Jae watched as Dal clicked something on screen. As he did, a group of archers fired arrows into a crowd of monsters on the battlefield.

Jae took a cautious step forward. She was almost afraid that her brother would spin and yell at her to get out. But she stayed focused on the computer screen. She couldn't quite understand what was happening in the game. But something about it seemed to grab her attention.

Then there was another explosion and Dal pulled off his headset in frustration. Jae could see his castle burning and his soldiers falling to their doom.

"You're not supposed to be in here," Dal said without turning around. "You can't sneak up on me like that. You totally messed me up!"

CHAPTER 3

SNEAKY SUBSTITUTE

Jae was shocked. She was in her brother's room and he hadn't thrown her out . . . yet. She found a spot on his bed where she could see what he was doing.

"You need to turn it . . ." Jae began, but her voice trailed off as Dal began building a new castle from scratch. "What are you playing?"

"*CASTLE CRUSADERS 5*. And no, you can't play," Dal said quickly. "You're too young to figure it out anyway."

"No, I'm not," Jae said, folding her arms in protest. "Being three years older doesn't mean you're better at games!"

"Whatever. I need to concentrate on this," Dal said.

"So do I," Jae said, crossing her arms. "I'm trying to do my homework and it sounds like the end of the world in here."

"It will be if I don't get better at this game," Dal said. "I won't get into the esports tournament if I can't even beat Tim."

Jae had met Tim. He wasn't her favorite person. But then again, none of Dal's friends were.

"Is it like chess?" Jae asked.

"Not exactly. More like chess on five energy drinks," Dal responded.

Jae thought about that. She'd played chess a few times and wasn't too bad at it. Of course, she'd never won a game, but she'd come close. Or at least, that's what she'd been told.

"Can you at least turn it down?" Jae said, remembering her homework. "Aren't you supposed to just listen through your headphones?"

Dal nodded and reached for the dial on his external speakers.

"I like the sound to play through my speakers too," he said. "That way it feels like I'm at the esports tournament. But here, I'll turn it down. Happy?"

Before Jae could respond, Dal put his headphones back on and began another round.

"Okay, Tim. Prepare to eat dirt!" he said into his microphone.

Jae resisted the urge to watch another round of *CASTLE CRUSADERS 5*. She stood up and backed out of Dal's room, never taking her eyes off the screen. Once in the hallway, she ran into her mother.

"Did he finally turn it down?" Mom asked. "And did he actually let you in there?"

"Yes, and, sort of," Jae replied. "Crazy, right?"

Mom smiled. "I'm just glad you two are finally getting along."

"I wouldn't go that far," Jae replied, heading back to her room. "Sorry, I need to finish my homework while there's a moment of quiet."

Jae sat down and got to work on her assignments. But the whole time she kept thinking about Dal playing his game. As if on cue, her brother groaned in dismay.

I guess things aren't going well, Jae thought.

After another ten minutes, she finished her Civil War assignment and stuck it in her folder. Then Jae turned and glanced toward the hallway. As she did, her mom appeared and opened Dal's door. Mom poked her head in and shouted.

"Dal!"

No response. After a moment she went in.

"Dal . . . DAL!"

He's wearing headphones, Mom, Jae thought,

then walked across the hall to watch. Mom reached out and grabbed Dal's shoulder, which nearly scared him out of his socks. Dal immediately pulled his headset off.

"WHOA! What? What did I do?"

Mom shook her head. "Don't you have to work tonight?"

In less than five seconds, Dal's face went from startled to annoyed to terrified. He jumped from his chair and sent it spinning like a top. Mom and Jae leaped out of the way as he ran to his dresser to grab his work shirt and name tag.

"Gotta go!" Dal cried, rushing out the door. He left both Jae and Mom in his room.

"I'm surprised Grocer's Value hasn't fired him yet," Mom said, leaving. "He's never on time!"

Jae stood alone in Dal's room. On the computer monitor, a new castle was ready to

be defended. Faint mumbling came from Dal's headphones.

As the spinning chair slowed to a stop, Jae stepped forward and sat at the desk.

She felt her heart beat quickly in her chest as she raised the headphones to her head.

"You still there, man?" a voice that sounded like Tim's asked. "We gonna do this or what?"

Jae scanned the screen, afraid to respond. Instead, she grabbed the mouse and clicked the ENGAGE button. Immediately the game came to life.

"Well, all right!" Tim chirped in her ear.

CHAPTER 4

BATTLE DAMAGE

Jae had no idea what she was doing, and Tim quickly celebrated his easy victory.

"I'm always four steps ahead of you, Cho," Tim said through the headset. He did that annoying thing boys do, calling people by their last name. Within minutes, he was cheering himself on as he toppled the castle Dal had built.

Jae almost said something but stopped herself. Her voice wouldn't sound like Dal's. Tim would tell Dal, and then she'd really be in trouble. Instead, she just stayed silent and watched as Tim's army of trolls invaded the ruins of the castle.

Despite being beaten, Jae couldn't help but smile. There was something about playing

CASTLE CRUSADERS 5 that she absolutely loved. It reminded her of when she and her brother used to play with plastic Blockos bricks. They had built a whole plastic city on the living room floor. While Dal had built the cars and police station, Jae created an entire mansion from scratch. Even Dal thought it was impressive.

I want to build something again, Jae thought, almost catching herself saying it out loud.

"One more match?" Tim asked. "Then I have to eat supper."

Afraid to speak, Jae clicked the RISE AGAIN button. The game moved to the CASTLE CONSTRUCT page where there were plenty of pieces to choose and build from. In the corner of the screen was a timer counting down from five minutes.

Five minutes? Jae thought. *That's too much pressure! How can anyone build a decent castle in five minutes?*

She scanned the screen, studying the pieces and dragging them to her plot on the map. Some of the corners didn't line up, and she dropped a few pieces where they wouldn't do her castle any good.

With the remaining minute, she placed her king and queen inside the shabby structure, hoping they'd be safe. She also positioned her soldiers wherever she could.

TIME'S UP! the screen said. LET'S GET READY TO CRUMBLE!

As the game began, she heard Tim in her headphones. "Three in a row," he said. "I can taste it now, Cho!"

Jae watched Tim's team move first. His troll archers fired arrows from his impressive castle walls. She cringed as a handful of her soldiers were taken out immediately. When it came to her turn, she realized she had her archers on the ground. As they fired their arrows, they bounced harmlessly off Tim's stone walls.

"It's like you've never played before!" Tim cried. A moment later, he launched a fiery tar ball from one of his catapults. Jae watched the front of her jumbled castle explode, leaving a giant hole in the front.

Three moves later, her royal family was captured and Tim's trolls were chasing the remaining soldiers off into the wilderness.

Jae sat back and shook her head. She could only watch the fires burn and the smoke billow from the husk of her poor, sad-looking castle. Then she quickly logged off the game.

"I have a lot to learn," Jae said aloud. Then a smile broke across her face. "And I can't wait."

*　*　*

In front of school the next morning, Jae ran into Bishara.

"I sneaked onto Dal's computer last night after he ran off to work. I played *CASTLE CRUSADERS 5* as him," Jae said in a whisper.

"Oooh," Bishara said. "He would lose it if he caught you!"

"Definitely," Jae said. "We barely get along as it is. But I couldn't just let his castle get destroyed without trying to help."

"So did you save the day?" Bishara asked.

"Nope," Jae said. "But it was fun trying."

"I'd be careful. Sneaking into an older brother's room is never a good idea."

"I know," Jae said opening the front door. "Maybe you and I should play against each other. We could both learn."

Bishara shook her head. "No thanks," she said. "I can't stand those real-time strategy games. They're so boring."

Blunt as always, Jae thought.

"That's okay," Jae said quickly. "That was probably the last time I'll get to play anyway. Dal's trying to get into an esports tournament or something. He'll be playing constantly."

CHAPTER 5

RESISTANCE IS FUTILE

At dinner that night, Jae eyed the empty spot where Dal usually sat.

"Where's Dal?" Jae asked.

"He's working a longer shift tonight," Mom said, handing her a bowl of kimchi. "He was warned about being late so many times. I think he's trying to earn some good worker points at the grocery store."

Jae nodded and added some vegetables to her plate. Her brother had gotten a job soon after he turned 16. She was a bit jealous of the money he was making. But she didn't like the idea of being stuck at work for hours on end.

While Dad and Mom talked about the day, Jae found herself rearranging the vegetables on her plate. She imagined them as small structures on a medieval battlefield. She set a piece of cabbage over the top as a makeshift roof and used a piece of fish as one of the battlements.

"Are you playing with your food, Jae?" her dad asked.

Jae looked up, startled.

"Oops," she said snatching up a piece from her structure to eat. "I guess so. Sorry!"

After finishing her meal, Jae grabbed a soda and went upstairs. She paused at Dal's bedroom door.

The *SUPER FIGHTERS* on Dal's sign seemed to dare her to go in his room.

No way, Jae thought. *As much as I want to play* CASTLE CRUSADERS 5, *that's just asking for trouble.*

Deciding her life wasn't worth risking, she went to her room. But she couldn't help but turn back to look at the two fighters that stared at her from across the hall.

Don't even think about it, Jae, the fighter with the black spiky hair seemed to say. *We'll turbo kick your butt right out of here.*

"You don't scare me," Jae said, and promptly walked over and opened Dal's bedroom door.

His room, as usual, was a giant mess. It looked like a clothes tornado had torn through the room. But Jae didn't pay attention to the clutter. She instead zeroed in on the glowing monitor at the other end of the room.

The screen displayed the game lobby for *CASTLE CRUSADERS 5.* Animated soldiers and trolls ran across the screen swinging swords and axes. The START button was pulsing, as if beckoning her to join the fight once more.

Her instincts told her not to, but Jae couldn't resist a good game. As if on autopilot,

she sat at her brother's desk, set down her soda can, and took a deep breath.

"Just one match," Jae said. Before she could talk herself out of it, Jae clicked START.

In no time, she logged in as her brother and saw a list of his online friends along the side of the screen. She looked for a way to play on her own so she could learn more, but before she had a chance, the screen changed.

A CHALLENGER APPROACHES! The screen said in bright, fiery letters: *TimzTrollz.*

Great, Jae thought. *So much for a tutorial!*

Reluctantly, Jae pulled the headset on.

"Hey, Dal," Tim said. "I thought you had to work tonight."

Jae froze. She almost tore the headset off and jumped offline.

"Hey, you there, Cho?" Tim asked impatiently. "Hello?"

CHAPTER 6

A CLOSE CALL

Jae sat frozen at the keyboard, unsure what to do next. She couldn't say anything or Tim would tell Dal she was playing on his computer.

Jae clicked an icon shaped like a keyboard. A little window that said MESSAGE MODE popped up. Hurriedly, she typed a quick note.

SORRY. MICROPHONE NOT WORKING.

"Dude!" Tim cried. "You just got that headset. Oh, well. At least I won't hear you crying when I kick your butt!"

Jae did her best to ignore Tim. Instead, she focused on building a castle with thick walls. She then added barriers in front of the main gate and placed soldiers in the field. She put her archers on top of the walls to defend the castle.

Suddenly, a spinning gold coin appeared on the screen. When it stopped with heads showing, Jae was given the first turn to attack.

Jae clicked on her left catapult to launch it, but frowned a bit. The tar ball wasn't on fire like Tim's was. The huge rock slammed into his wall, but it didn't do nearly as much damage as she hoped.

"Saving your power-ups for later, eh?" Tim cackled in her ear. "Too bad there won't *be* a later after my trolls begin their siege!"

Power-ups? Jae thought. She looked at her options and saw symbols with fire, ice, some sort of green gloop, and a cluster of monkeys. None of it made any sense to her, but she wanted to learn . . . and quickly.

In no time, Tim had sent his trolls onto the battlefield. They all held axes with a weird, green glow. As the monsters hacked their way closer to her castle, she saw her soldiers fall over with green bubbles coming off them.

"Did he just poison my men?" Jae whispered aloud. She quickly clamped her hand over her mouth.

"What did you say?" Tim asked. "Hey, I think your mic is working, Cho!"

Jae quickly typed another message.

NOT SURE WHAT THAT WAS DUDE.

On her next move, Jae sent out her army of soldiers to face off against the trolls. They cut through the monsters and stormed the front of Tim's castle.

"I knew you'd fall for that," Tim said. "Always four steps ahead of you, man."

Jae blinked and watched as five giant fireballs were launched from his hidden catapults. She slowly shook her head and mouthed *NOOOO* as the attack smashed her little castle to pieces. In a matter of minutes, her game was over.

Even so, Jae smiled. She was learning.

LET'S GO AGAIN.

*   *   *

One more game turned into two games. And then two games became almost ten. Jae found herself understanding a little more with each match. But every time, Tim pulled out some random attack she never saw coming.

Out of curiosity, Jae clicked on the button marked CLUSTER-OF-MONKEYS. She watched and covered a laugh as the catapult flung a bunch of shrieking monkeys through the air onto Tim's castle.

"One of the dumbest additions to this game ever," Tim said. "No one uses it because they don't do any damage. I hope they take them out of *CASTLE CRUSADERS 6*. Weak!"

Jae watched as the trolls kicked the monkeys off the towers. They screeched and ran off into the surrounding forests.

She held her breath as a wizard appeared on top of Tim's right tower. The old, bearded troll raised his hand to the sky and icy darts appeared from the animated clouds above.

"Prepare for thy icy doom!" Tim screeched. "Esports Strategy Showdown, here I come!"

As the first volley of icy daggers dropped, Jae heard a car pull into the driveway.

She looked at the clock. It was nearly 9:00 p.m.

Uh, oh. That means . . . Dal is home!

Without knowing what else to do, Jae hit the ESC key on the keyboard. The screen said ARE YOU SURE YOU WANT TO QUIT?

"Yes," Jae said, tearing off her headphones and clicking on SURE I'M SURE.

She stood up as she heard her brother's feet on the stairs. With no time to lose, Jae turned off the monitor and ran out the door.

CHAPTER 7

SOFT DRINK SNEAK

Jae flopped onto her bed and pulled her phone out of her pocket. She pretended to look at it intently as Dal made his way to his room.

"Hey Dal," Jae called from her room. "How was work?"

Her brother turned and looked at her like she was some sort of alien creature.

"Um . . . okay," he replied, shaking his head. "Actually, that's not true. It was pretty terrible. Jeremy never showed up and we were super busy."

"Oh, that *is* terrible," Jae replied.

"You're acting weird," he said. Then he turned and looked at his partially opened bedroom door. "Were you in my room?"

Jae felt her eyes go wide. She stayed perfectly still and just stared at her phone's blank screen, frozen in fear.

"I don't think so," she said. The lie felt sour on her tongue. "Not since last night."

"You don't *think* so. Right. Great answer," Dal said. Then he went in his room, leaving the door open.

Oh, boy, Jae thought. *That was awful.*

She reached to her night stand for her soda can. Finding nothing there, she panicked.

My drink! I left it in Dal's room!

Jae stood up and paced around her bed. How could she have forgotten the soda? Would Dal be mad when he saw it?

Unsure what to do, Jae went to Dal's open door. She peered in to see her brother rummaging through his backpack. Glancing to the left, she saw the can of Tangy Treat sitting next to Dal's keyboard.

Great, she thought.

"Are you playing *CASTLE CRUSADERS 5* tonight?" Jae asked.

She wondered if Tim was mad that she jumped out of the game before his wizard could destroy her castle for the ninth time.

"Nope. I've got homework coming out of my ears," Dal replied with a frustrated grunt. "I'm supposed to be preparing for the Esports Strategy Showdown. I totally stink and have no time to practice."

"Oh, that's too bad," Jae said, keeping her eye on the soda can.

"It doesn't matter," Dal said. "Tim will probably win anyway."

Jae slowly moved closer to the desk, freezing anytime Dal paused from digging through his bag. He took out a textbook and a few notebooks, and then tossed the backpack onto the floor.

"Where is that stupid schedule?" Dal asked, as if some of his mess might magically move on its own to reveal it. "I don't even know if I'm working tomorrow."

Jae reached for the soda can just as Dal turned toward his desk.

"What are you doing in here?" Dal demanded.

Jae gulped and stood up straight, clasping her hands behind her back.

"I thought you might want something to drink if you were going to play your game," Jae said, thinking quickly.

"Uh, huh," Dal said, looking over at the can on his desk. "Right. So, you're just sneaking a soda in?"

"It was kind of fun watching you play that game," Jae replied quickly. "I thought if I was nice, maybe you'd let me watch again."

Dal took a deep breath and let it out.

"Yeah, whatever," he said, looking confused. "Thanks for that, but I can't tonight. Between my homework and work-work, I'm probably not getting into the tournament anyway."

"Oh, okay," Jae said. "Well, maybe next time."

"Right," Dal said. "Now get out of here."

Jae scurried off. She didn't need to be told twice.

CHAPTER 8

SATURDAY SLIP-UP

Saturday morning found Jae with her
WORD NERDS game app open again. Bishara
was waiting for her to move, but sent her a
message through the game's chat feature.

U STILL THERE? STILL THINKING?

I'm still here, Jae thought, lying in bed and
staring at the ceiling. *But I'm not thinking about
this dumb spelling game.*

She looked at the letters she had left: A, S,
T, Y.

I don't care about finding words right now,
Jae decided. In fact, she wasn't sure she'd ever
care about *WORD NERDS* again. She gave up
and pushed the SURRENDER button, letting
Bishara win again.

Her phone rang almost immediately. It was Bishara, wanting to do a VidChat. Jae clicked the button, showing her friend's confused face.

"Okay, what happened?" Bishara asked. "You could have spelled a bunch of words. I actually thought you were going to beat me today."

"Yeah," Jae said. "You're probably right, but I think I'm done playing *WORD NERDS*."

Bishara smirked. "It's your brother's game, isn't it? That castle fighter one."

"Yeah," she admitted. "But I have to be done with that one, too. I got way too close to getting caught last night. I had to dive out of his room at the last second!"

"Oooof," Bishara said. "He would NOT be happy to find you messing with his game."

Jae nodded. She could only imagine how much Dal would yell at her if he knew what she'd been up to.

"So what are you doing today?" Jae asked. "Want to go see a movie or something? I need to get out of the house."

Bishara frowned. "I wish I could," she said. "But I'm helping my parents at the store for a few hours this morning. Maybe after lunch when I get home?"

"Sure," Jae said. "That works. Let me know."

The two of them said goodbye and disconnected. But as soon as she did, Jae realized how quiet the house was. She swung her legs out from under the covers and went downstairs. The kitchen was empty, and she found a note from her parents.

WENT SHOPPING. DAL IS AT WORK. WE'LL BE BACK SOON! LOVE MOM AND DAD.

Great, Jae thought. *Home alone with nothing to do.*

She turned and stared at the stairs leading up to hers and Dal's bedrooms.

Well, almost *nothing to do,* Jae thought.

Five minutes later, Jae was behind the keyboard in Dal's room, logging into *CASTLE CRUSADERS 5.* As she did, several annoying windows popped up. She ignored what they said, hitting "ACCEPT" on one and "I AGREE" on another. She just wanted to get on with playing the game.

Inside the game lobby, things looked a little different. There were a bunch of player names that Jae didn't recognize. It took her a moment to realize they weren't Dal's friends. They were other online players. But as soon as she put on the headphones, she heard a familiar voice.

"Can't believe you bailed on me last night, Cho," Tim said. "Just couldn't take the pressure, huh?"

Jae remembered jumping out of the game as Tim unleashed some sort of wizard attack she'd never seen before. She wondered if that completely forfeited the game for her brother.

Jae opened up the game's MESSAGE MODE and typed in:

SORRY ABOUT THAT.

"Headset still isn't working?" Tim said. "You need to throw out that piece of junk. Today's the big day. Good luck, Dal!"

Jae wrinkled her eyebrows in confusion. *Big day?* She thought. *What's he talking about?*

Jae scanned the screen and saw there were a bunch of changes to the game. There was a large point counter up near Dal's user name: *DalForReal2004.* She'd never seen *CASTLE CRUSADERS 5* keep track of points before.

What's going on here? Jae wondered.

As if in answer, a loud adult voice came on through her headset.

"Welcome to the *CASTLE CRUSADERS 5* Esports Strategy Showdown qualifying round!"

Uh, oh! Jae thought.

CHAPTER 9

READY, SET, ATTACH!

Every instinct in Jae's body told her to click the QUIT button, turn off the screen, and run and hide in her room. Maybe Dal would never find out. Maybe she could find some new game to keep her interested.

Even so, Jae didn't move. The announcer's voice seemed to cast a spell over her.

"You've entered into the realm of battle, magic, and catapult chaos," the announcer said. "Here you'll match wits against other warriors in a fierce battle of firepower and strategy."

On the screen, animated trolls and soldiers got into position as if they were part of the program. One ugly troll even wore a tuxedo and hid a battle axe behind his back.

"Here, instead of victory, you'll be battling for points. Rack up enough points, and you'll move up our leader board," the announcer said. "The two warriors with the most points will battle to win a spot in this fall's Esports Strategy Showdown tournament!"

Jae nodded. *Points, points, points. Got it.*

"Ready, set, ATTACK!" the announcer said.

Immediately, the game dumped Jae into a pre-built castle. She launched her soldiers forward to attack her opponent's army of trolls. Her little soldiers fought hard, racking up points on the board. Then she readied her catapult with a powered-up FIRERAIN attack.

"Fire!" Jae shouted into the microphone.

"Wait! Wait!" her opponent cried.

Jae didn't wait. She launched the attack and watched as three beautiful fireballs soared across the battlefield to destroy the enemy's catapults. Points racked up on the screen.

"REALLY? You wrecked my catapults and not my castle?" her opponent shouted.

Before Jae could respond, she was dropped into another prebuilt castle against a new foe. She glanced up at the score and saw she already had close to 100,000 points.

Is that good? Jae wondered. Either way, she was in too deep to turn back now.

Jae let her new opponent, *KingKlasher12,* take turns attacking her castle. Meanwhile, she prepped her wizard with LIGHTNING LASH LEVEL 3.

When the attack was ready, Jae unleashed a storm to end all storms. Jagged bolts of lightning shot from her wizard's hands and tore through KingKlasher's castle, blowing the rocks to rubble.

An announcement on the screen said TRIPLE POINTS. Jae couldn't help but squeal with excitement. She just wished she could do that sort of damage against Tim.

As the morning wore on, Jae put more points on the board as she battled nearly a dozen players. At just under 700,000 points, the screen suddenly froze and the words STOP THE SIEGE appeared.

"Uh, oh," Jae whispered. "Is that it?"

"The battle is over," the announcer said. "And there can be only two."

A drumroll played through the headset as the game prepared to announce the finalists. Jae looked to see if anything showed the other players' scores. There wasn't. But a moment later, she got her answer . . .

"Prepare for battle *DalforReal2004 and TimzTrollz!*"

"Good luck, Cho," Tim cackled through the headset. "You're going to need it."

CHAPTER 10

FIVE STEPS AHEAD

Jae watched as the screen changed, dropping her and Tim into castle-building mode. She scrambled to build her castle, trying something different.

She built small walls around her weapons for protection. Next, she strengthened her castle walls with another layer of stone. Finally, she placed her archers along the ramparts and hid her soldiers behind smaller stone walls. In no time at all, the words Jae had grown to love appeared on screen.

LET'S GET READY TO CRUMBLE!

Tim was given the first move. He launched his trolls onto the battlefield. Jae sent her soldiers out to clash with the filthy beasts.

On Tim's next turn, he readied a catapult to attack. "Cooking up something big and nasty for you, Cho," Tim warned. "You're going to love it."

I doubt that, Jae thought.

She scrolled through her list of attacks. Catapults, wizards, arrow volley. None of them seemed good enough. There was nothing that Tim wouldn't expect. As she scrolled to the end, she saw an attack that made her smile.

Can I use that, but power it up with fire? Jae wondered. She shrugged and tried it.

"Boom!" Tim shouted as he launched FIREBALL LEVEL 2. The first layer of Jae's castle crumbled away and Tim cackled in delight.

Jae launched a weak catapult attack and watched as the rocks did little damage to Tim's tower.

"Remember," Tim said. "I'm always four steps ahead of you, Dal."

Jae took a deep breath and watched as her special attack powered up. When it said READY she clicked the button.

The catapult launched a dozen monkeys into the air from Jae's castle. As they reached the top of their flight path, the monkeys pulled flaming torches out with their little paws.

FIERY MONKEY MODE! the game announced.

"What?" Tim cried. "That's not fair, I . . ."

Jae watched as the monkeys landed like little hairy ninjas, setting fire to everything. Tim's trolls ran with their rear-ends on fire. Catapults burned until they were useless. Even the king and queen ran across the battlefield as the monkeys chased them.

Tim spent his next turn trying to rebuild his catapults and put out the flames. But as he did, Jae powered up something "special" for him.

When the attack was ready, Jae launched ICE STORM LEVEL 3. She watched as Tim's castle and army were completely covered in ice. With Tim's forces frozen in place, Jae unleashed FIREBALL LEVEL 4 and demolished his castle. Within moments, she had captured victory.

"*Five* steps ahead, Tim!" Jae shouted into the microphone. "By the way, this is Jae, Dal's little sister!"

She heard Tim screech in horror as his defeat flashed across the screen.

DalforReal2004 WINS!

"Yes!" Jae shouted. She stood up and did a victory dance. But as she turned, she saw Dal standing there. His mouth hung open in shock.

"What did you do?" Dal said. He pointed to the computer. "Did . . . did you . . .?"

Jae stopped dancing. She tried to stop smiling, but couldn't. She'd won her first game in forever, and there was no way to hide it.

"I got you qualified for the Esports tournament," Jae replied. "Sorry, sort of, . . . and, uh, good luck?"

Dal shook his head. He looked completely confused and speechless.

"I . . . I can't believe it," Dal stammered.

"Are you angry?" Jae asked, waiting for her brother to start shouting and yelling at her.

"You're usually terrible at games," Dal said.

"Yeah, well, not this one I guess," Jae confessed.

Dal smiled and hugged his sister, which nearly made her fall over in shock.

"Good," Dal said, laughing. "Because you'll need to bring your A-game to the tournament!"

Jae's eyes widened as her brother squeezed her tight. She hugged him back.

Whoa, she thought. *Is he for real? He wants* ME *to compete in the tournament?!*

MORE ABOUT ESPORTS

- The first esports competition took place at Stanford University in October 1972. Students there competed in a game called *Spacewar*. The grand prize was a year-long subscription to *Rolling Stone* magazine.

- An estimated 474 million people watched esports events in 2021.

- The biggest esports game is *Dota 2*. It stands for *Defense of the Ancients 2* and is a multiplayer online battle arena (MOBA) game.

- The game *Utopia* for the Intellivision home console was released in 1981. It was the first Real Time Strategy (RTS) game ever released.

- RTS games come in all shapes and sizes. Some imitate historic military battles, while others are set in distant science fiction galaxies. Some fantasy RTS games are even based on the popular Lord of the Rings books and movies.

- There is some confusion between RTS and MOBA games. They are similar, but MOBA games focus more on a small group of heroes instead of an entire army.

- Esports teams usually practice together for eight hours a day, seven days a week. That's longer than a full-time, 40 hour-per-week job. Many players spend even more time practicing on their own time.

- A research study showed that during esports competitions, players had heart rates around 160–180 beats per minute. That's about the same as running a mile as fast as you can.

- Being an esports athlete isn't just about sitting in a chair with a controller or keyboard. The best competitors also exercise to train their body and mind and to sharpen their reflexes. Stretching and upper body exercises help keep esports athletes healthy!

TALK ABOUT IT

1. Jae and Dal are siblings who don't get along well at the beginning of the story. Why do you think this is? After the end of the story, do you think they'll be nicer to each other?

2. Bishara is Jae's best friend, but she doesn't seem very supportive or nice. Do you think she's mean on purpose? Should she let Jae win the *WORD NERDS* game once in a while? Discuss how these two could be best friends.

3. Jae is sneaky about playing her brother's *CASTLE CRUSADERS 5* game. Should she have admitted to Dal earlier that she was playing his game? Would Dal have been mad? Explain what you would have done in Jae's situation.

WRITE ABOUT IT

1. Jae suggests that she and Bishara should try playing *CASTLE CRUSADERS 5*, but Bishara isn't interested. However, consider what would happen if they did play the game together. Write about what would happen in the game. Would Bishara be any good? Would Jae finally beat her at a game?

2. Tim finds out he was beaten by Jae in the esports qualifying round. Write about what happens at Tim's house after he learns he wasn't actually playing against Dal. Would he be angry? Would he quit playing *CC5* for good?

3. Jae played well enough to qualify for the Esports Strategy Showdown tournament, and Dal wants her to keep going. Write about what happens next. How does Jae do in the tournament? Is she in over her head, or does she win the championship?

GLOSSARY

battlements (BAT-uhl-muhnts)—spaces on top of a castle's walls from which archers and soldiers fight to defend the castle

catapult (KAT-uh-puhlt)—a large weapon used to hurl rocks, flaming balls, or other dangerous objects at an enemy

forfeit (FOR-fuht)—to give up or lose a competition because of breaking a rule

kimchi (KIM-chee)—a spicy food from Korea made from fermented cabbage and other vegetables

leader board (LEE-dur BORD)—a board or list showing the scores of the leading competitors

MOD (MAHD)—short for modification; custom-made items, levels, or settings within a video game

ramparts (RAM-part)—the surrounding wall of a fort or castle built to protect against attacks

siege (SEEJ)—an attack on a castle, fort, or other protected location, meant to cut it off from supplies or help

tutorial (too-TOHR-ee-uhl)—a program designed to teach someone how to use a computer program or game

volley (VOL-ee)—an attack made by firing multiple weapons at an enemy at the same time

ABOUT THE AUTHOR

Thomas Kingsley Troupe is the author of a big ol' pile of books for kids. He's written about everything from ghosts to Bigfoot to 3rd grade werewolves. He even wrote a book about dirt. When he's not writing or reading, he gets plenty of exercise, plays video games, and remembers sacking quarterbacks while on his high school football team. Thomas lives in Woodbury, Minnesota with his two sons.

ABOUT THE ILLUSTRATOR

Fran Bueno is a comic artist with over 25 years of experience. He graduated in Fine Arts from the Complutense University of Madrid and has worked on illustrations for pamphlets, advertisements, children's books, and young adult comics. Fran also teaches traditional inking and graphic skills at the O Garaxe Hermético Professional School of Comics. He lives in Santiago de Compostela, Spain.

JAKE MADDOX eSPORTS
READ THEM ALL!

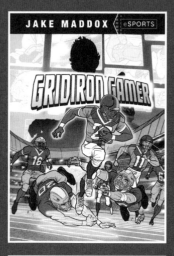